# Emily Gravett
# BEAR & HARE
## Where's Bear?

Simon & Schuster Books for Young Readers
NEW YORK  LONDON  TORONTO  SYDNEY  NEW DELHI

Bear and Hare are playing hide-and-seek.

6 7 8 9 10

Where's Bear?

There!

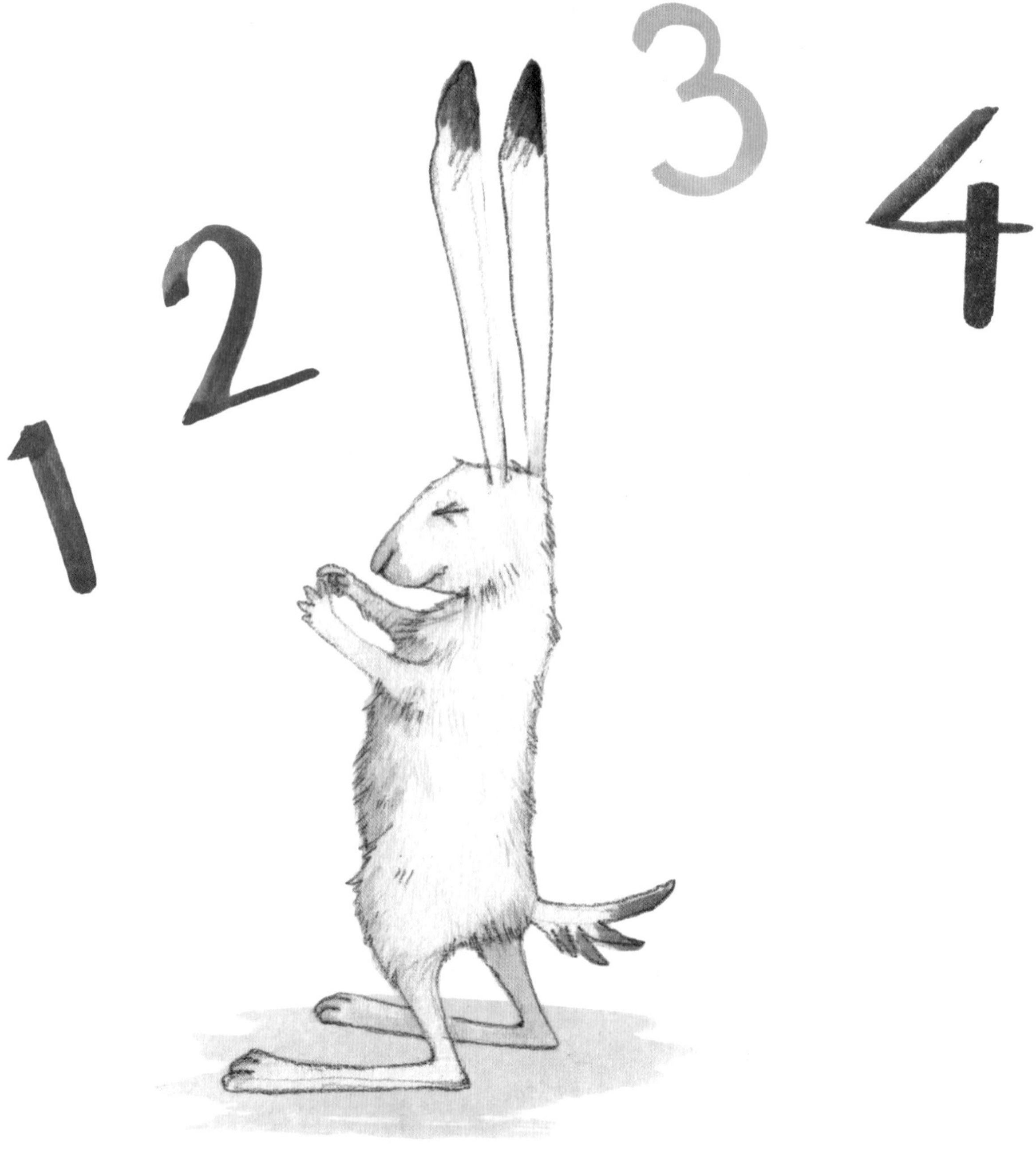
1 2 3 4

5 6 7 8 9 10

Where's Bear?

There.

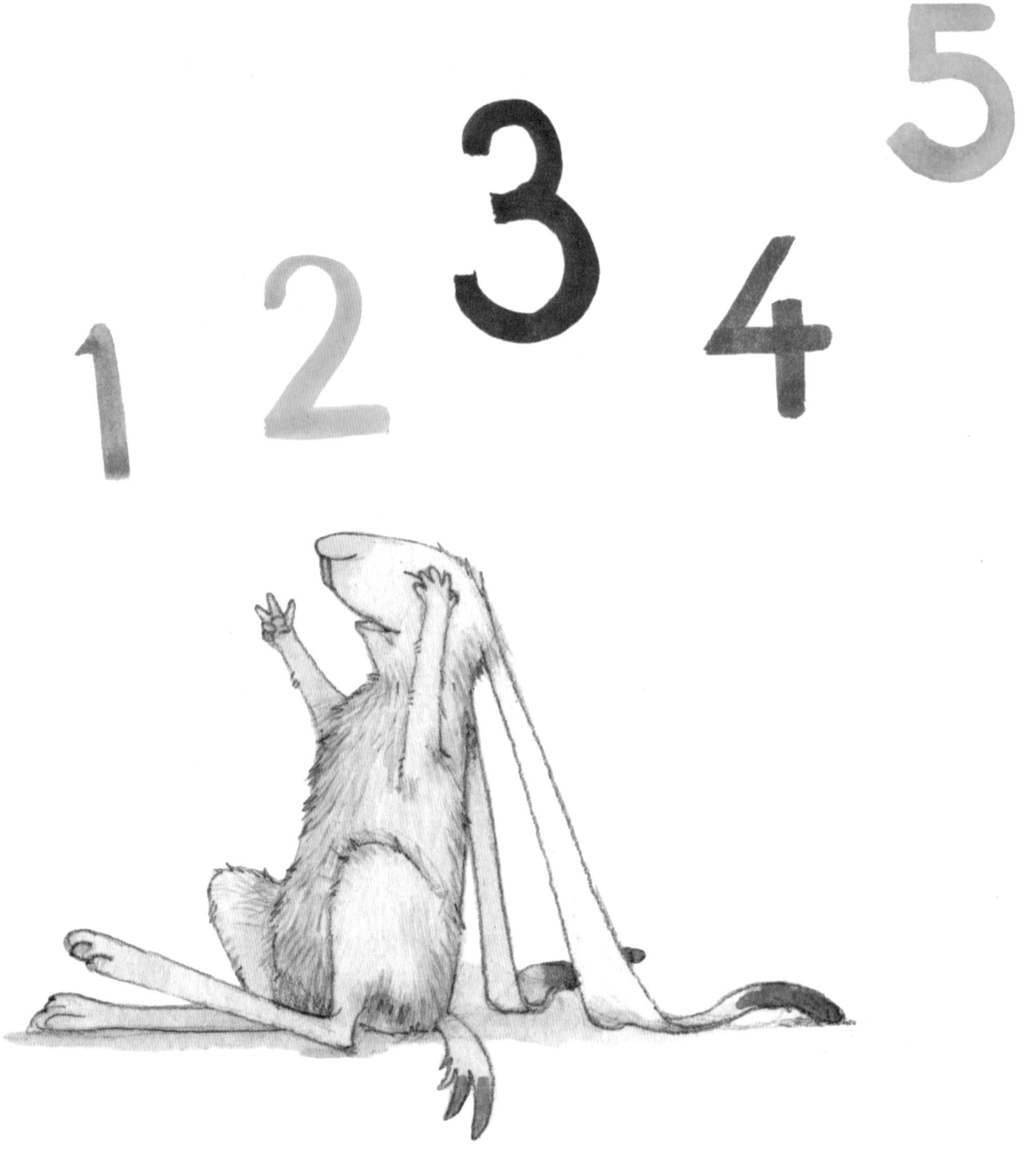
1
2
3
4
5

6 7 8 9 10

Where's Bear?

Oh, Bear!

Maybe Hare should try hiding instead?

4 5 6 7

8 9 10

Where's Hare?

Is he inside the teapot?

No.

Under the rug?

No!

Behind the picture?

NO!

Maybe Hare is under the blanket?

Where's Bear?

Is he under the
lamp shade?

No.

Behind
the books?

No!

In the fish tank?

NO!

Where IS Bear?

WANT BEAR!

There!

SIMON & SCHUSTER BOOKS FOR YOUNG READERS
An imprint of Simon & Schuster Children's Publishing Division
1230 Avenue of the Americas, New York, New York 10020
Copyright © 2014 by Emily Gravett
Originally published in 2014 in Great Britain by Macmillan Children's Books.
First US edition 2016
All rights reserved, including the right of reproduction in whole or in part in any form.
SIMON & SCHUSTER BOOKS FOR YOUNG READERS is a trademark of Simon & Schuster, Inc.
For information about special discounts for bulk purchases, please contact Simon & Schuster Special Sales at 1-866-506-1949 or business@simonandschuster.com.
The Simon & Schuster Speakers Bureau can bring authors to your live event. For more information or to book an event,
contact the Simon & Schuster Speakers Bureau at 1-866-248-3049 or visit our website at www.simonspeakers.com.
The text for this book is set in Pastonchi. • The illustrations for this book are rendered in pencil, watercolor, and wax crayons.
Manufactured in China • 1215 MCM
2 4 6 8 10 9 7 5 3 1
Library of Congress Cataloging-in-Publication Data
Gravett, Emily, author, illustrator.
Bear & Hare, where's Bear? / Emily Gravett.
pages cm
Summary: Friends Bear and Hare play a game of hide-and-seek, counting from one to ten each round.
ISBN 978-1-4814-5615-9 (hardcover)
ISBN 978-1-4814-5616-6 (eBook)
[1. Hide-and-seek—Fiction. 2. Friendship—Fiction. 3. Bears—Fiction. 4. Hares—Fiction. 5. Counting—Fiction.]
I. Title. II. Title: Bear and Hare, where's Bear?
PZ7.G77577Bi 2016
[E]—dc23
2015005866